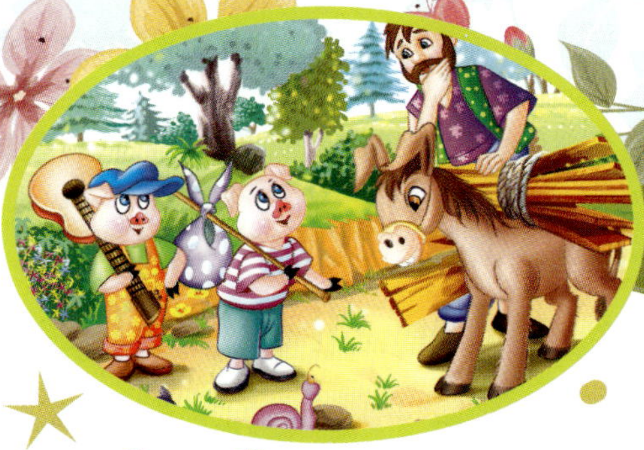

10 Minutes Fairy Tales

The Three Little Pigs

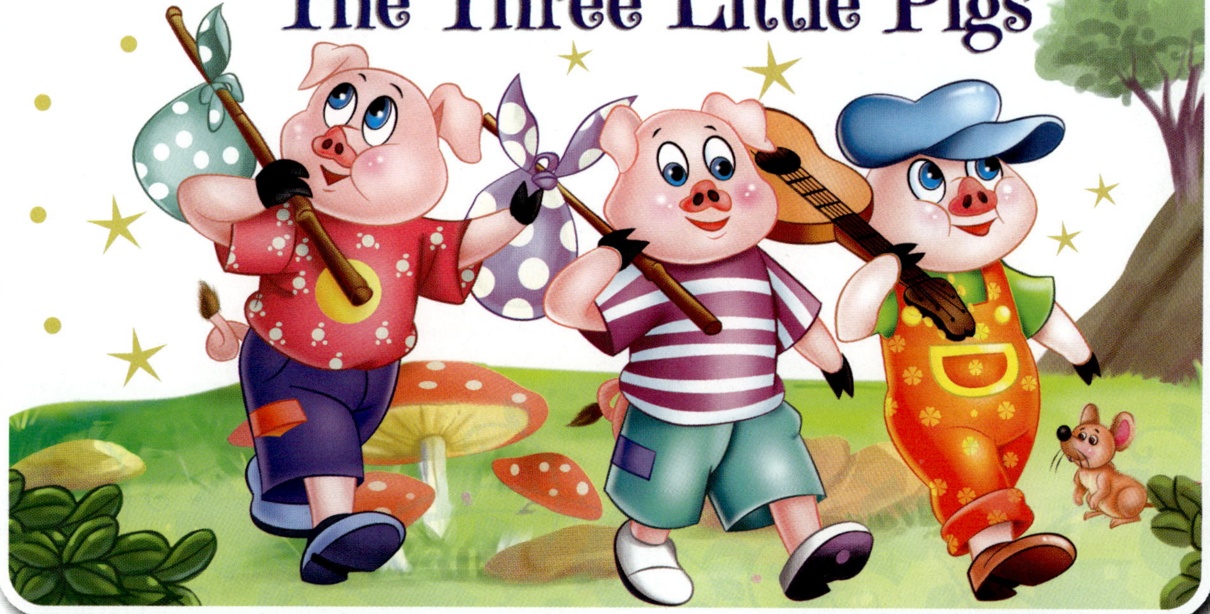

Once upon a time,
there lived a pig with her three little sons. The little pigs played all day long and had lots of fun. One day, the pig's mother said, "Now that you have grown too big, you all should go and build your own houses and learn the way of life." Agreeing to their mother's suggestion, they bid her goodbye.

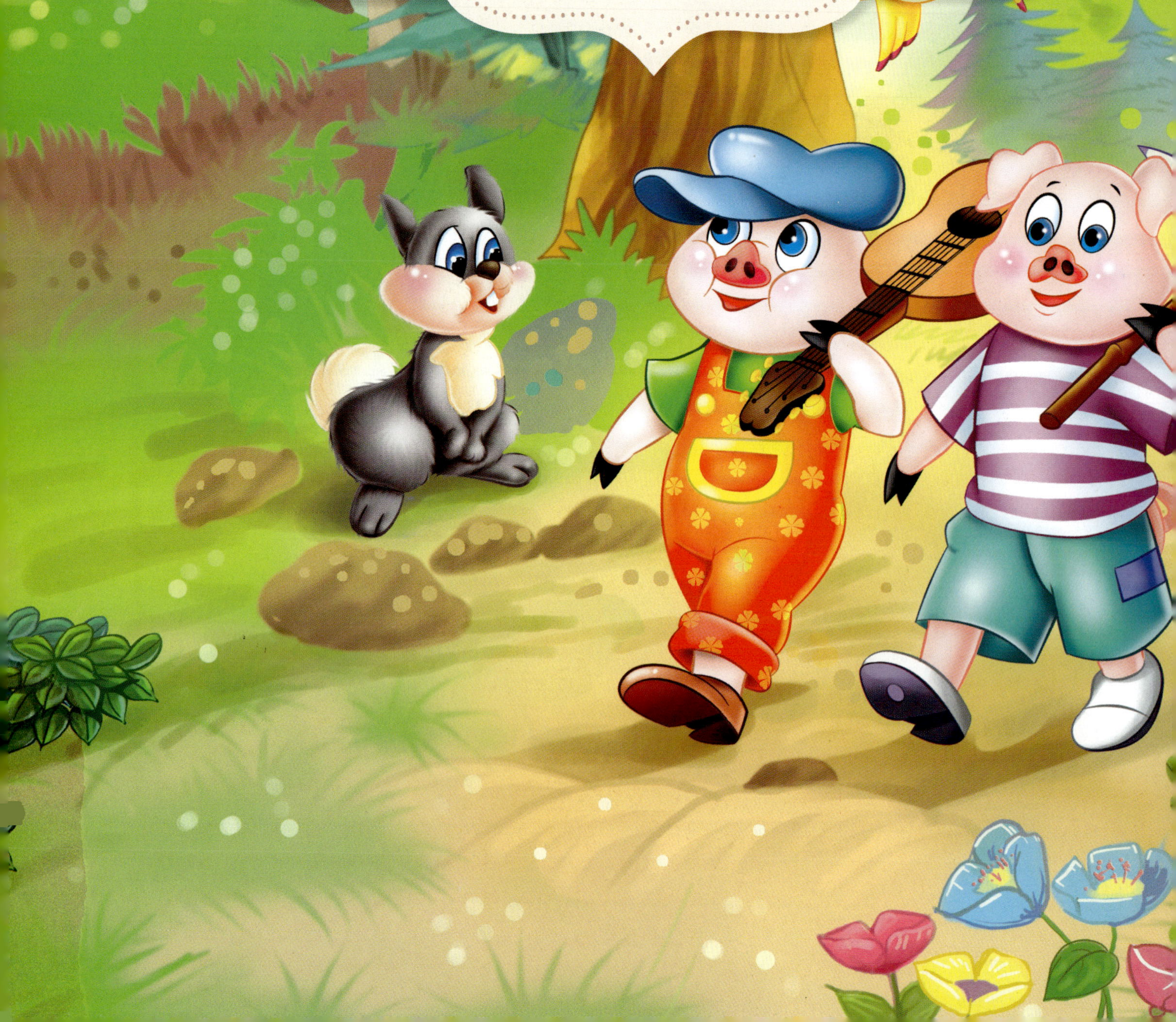

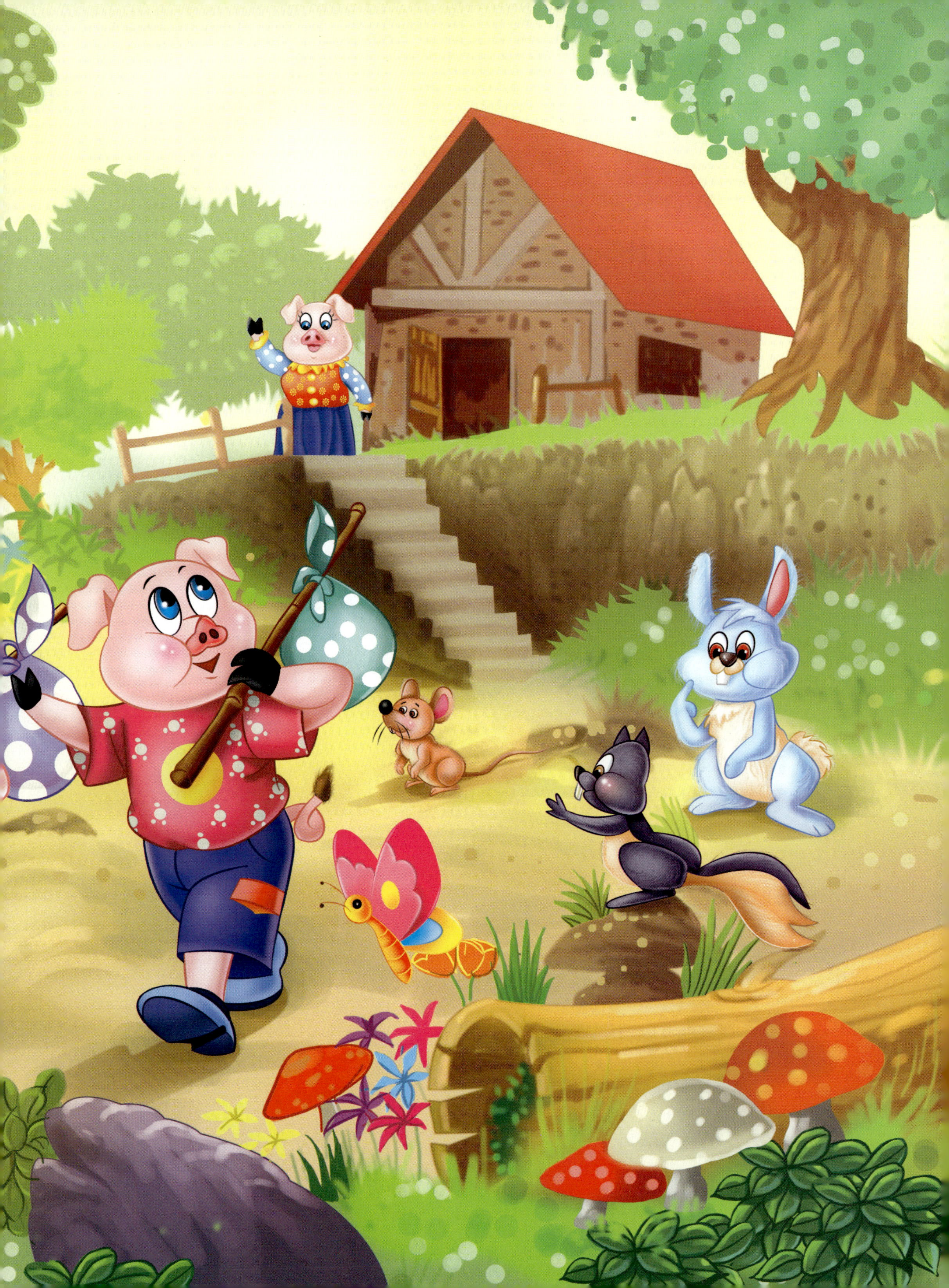

While on their way, the
first pig saw a man carrying a heap of straw.
The pig thought it would be a good idea to build a
house of straw, as it would be easily and quickly made.
So the pig bought the straw from the man and built
a house of straw for himself. He felt happy to have
built his home in no time.

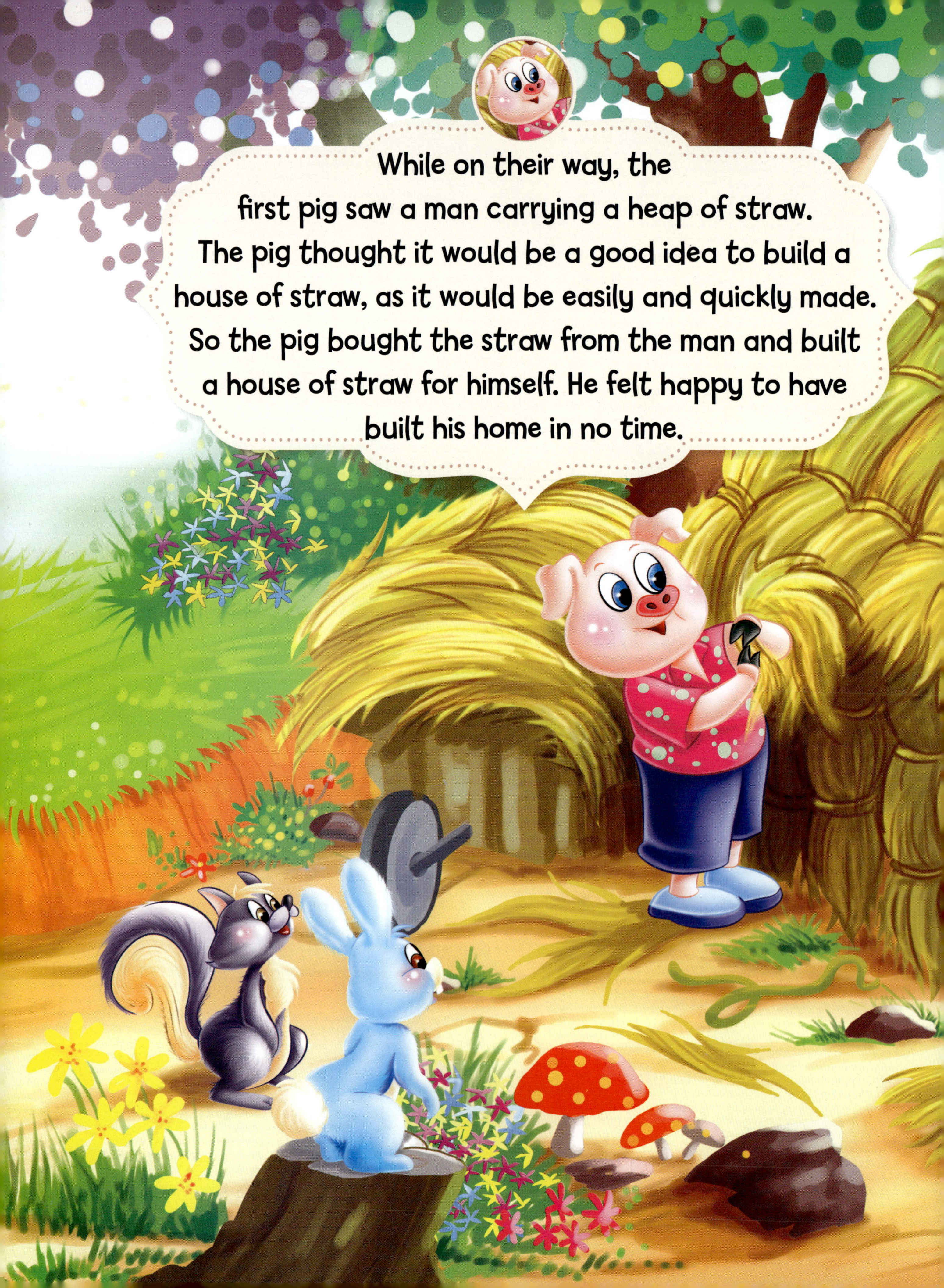

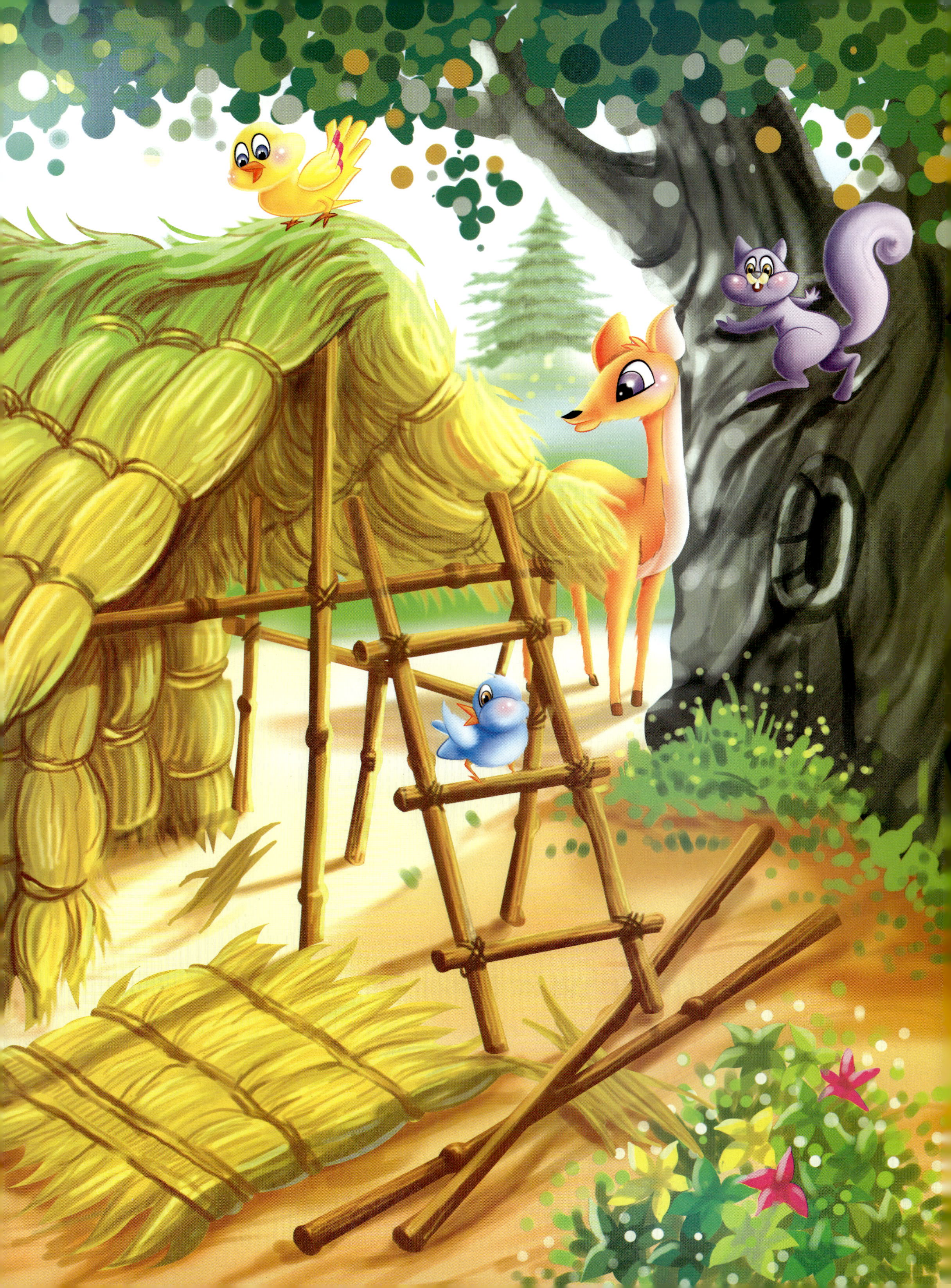

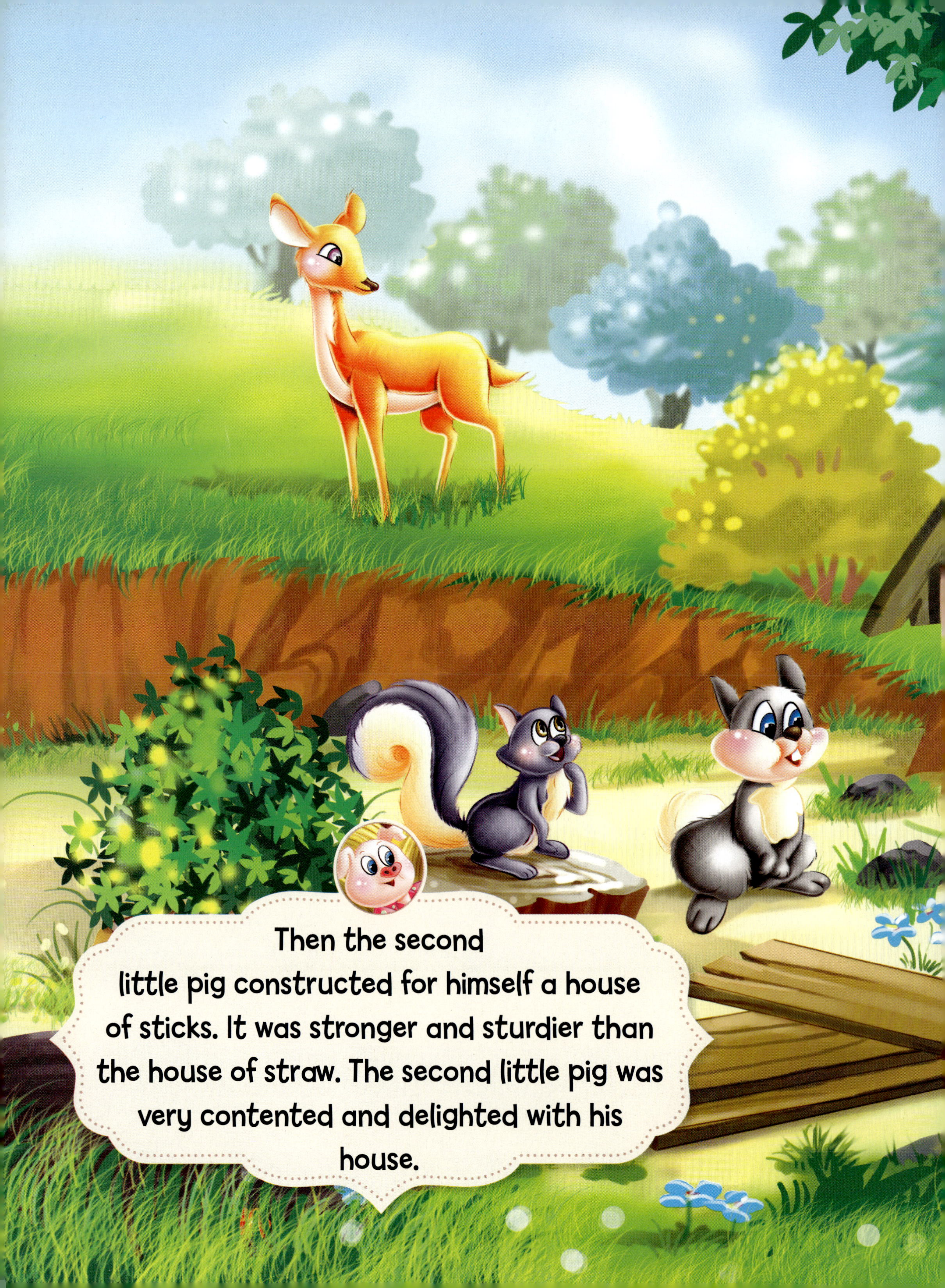

Then the second little pig constructed for himself a house of sticks. It was stronger and sturdier than the house of straw. The second little pig was very contented and delighted with his house.

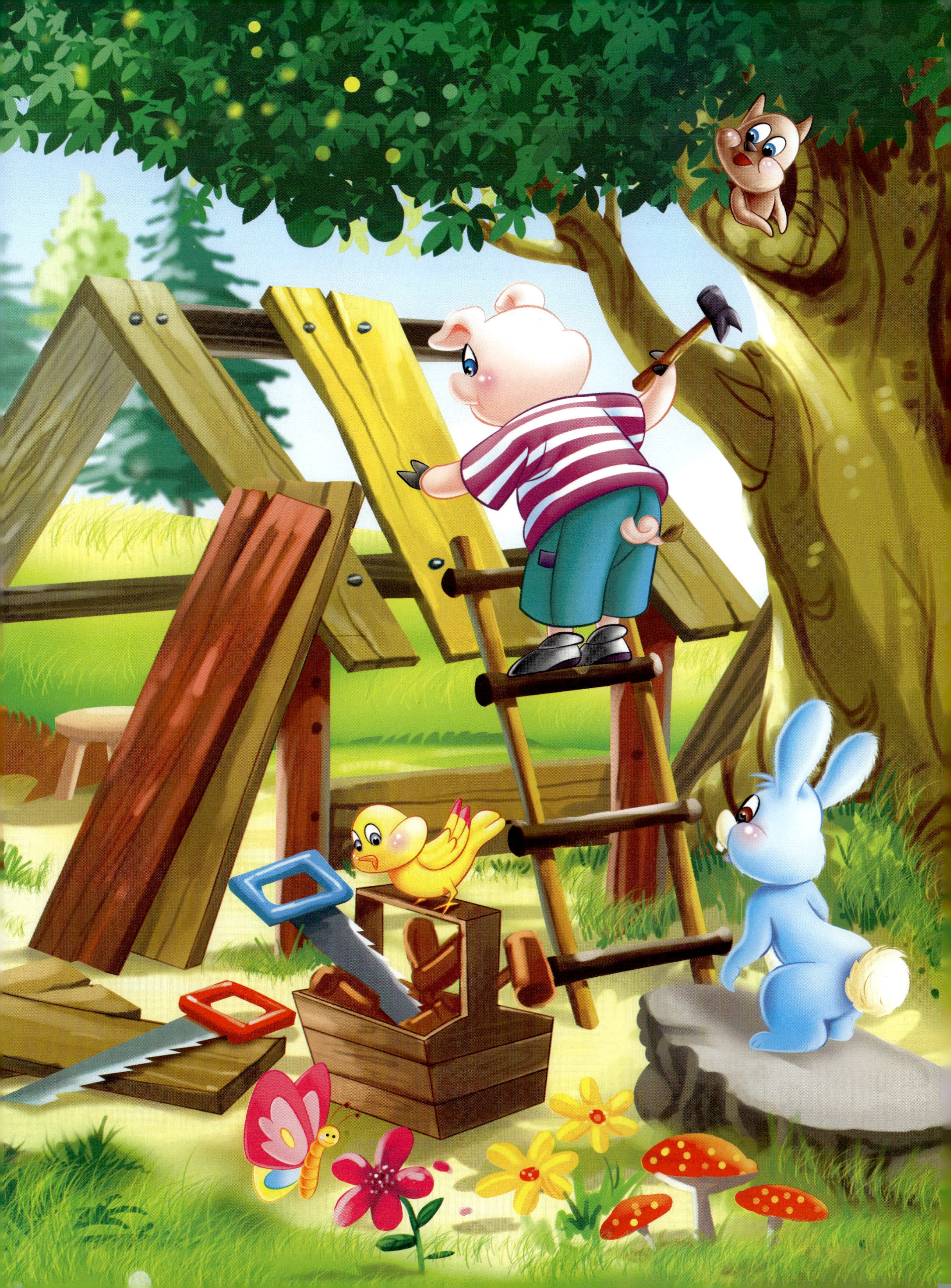

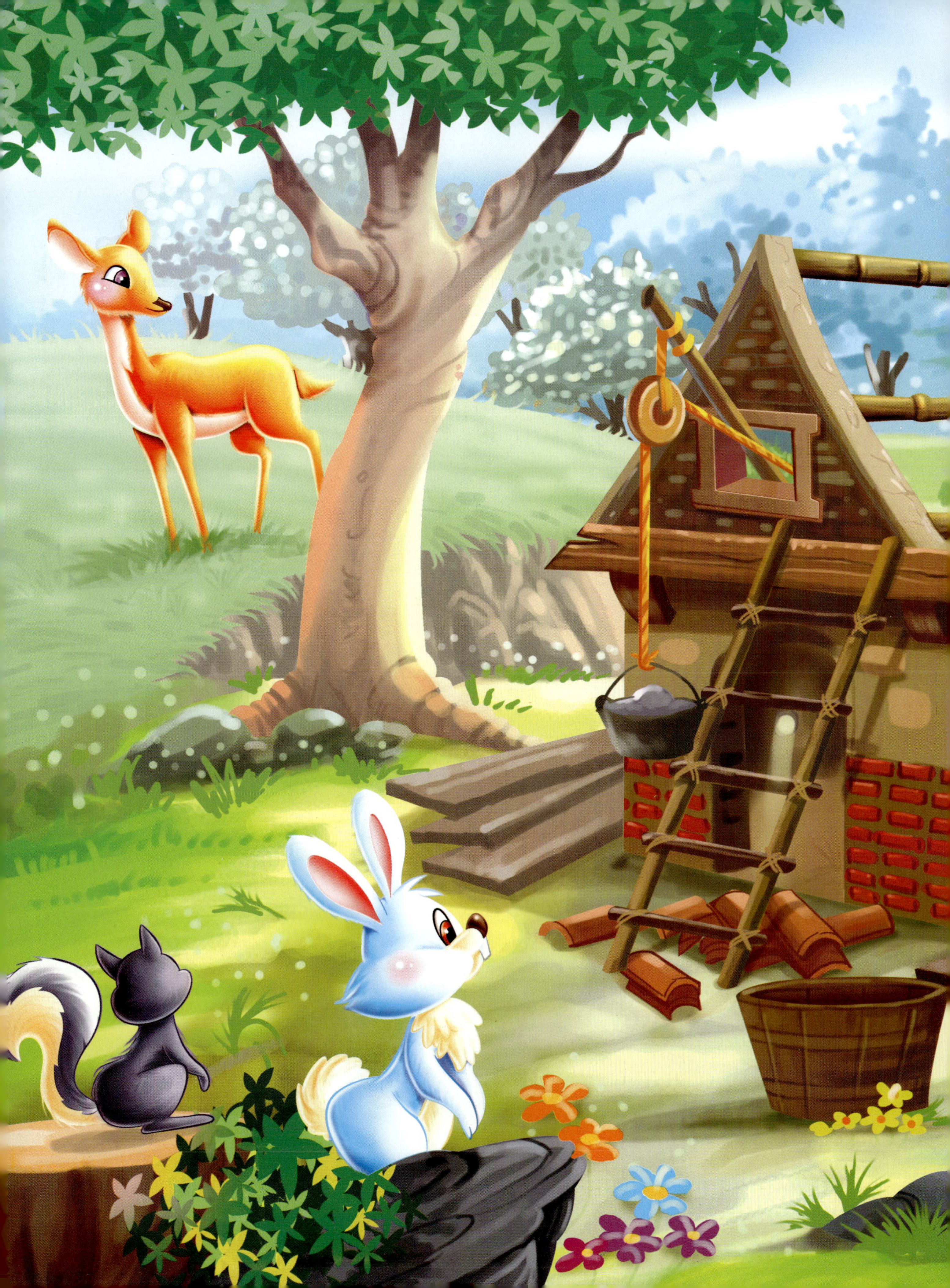

The third little pig built for himself a beautiful and strong house of bricks. He took a lot of time to build the house. “Now the wolf won’t be able to catch and eat me,” said the third little pig. All three little pigs were very happy with their own houses.

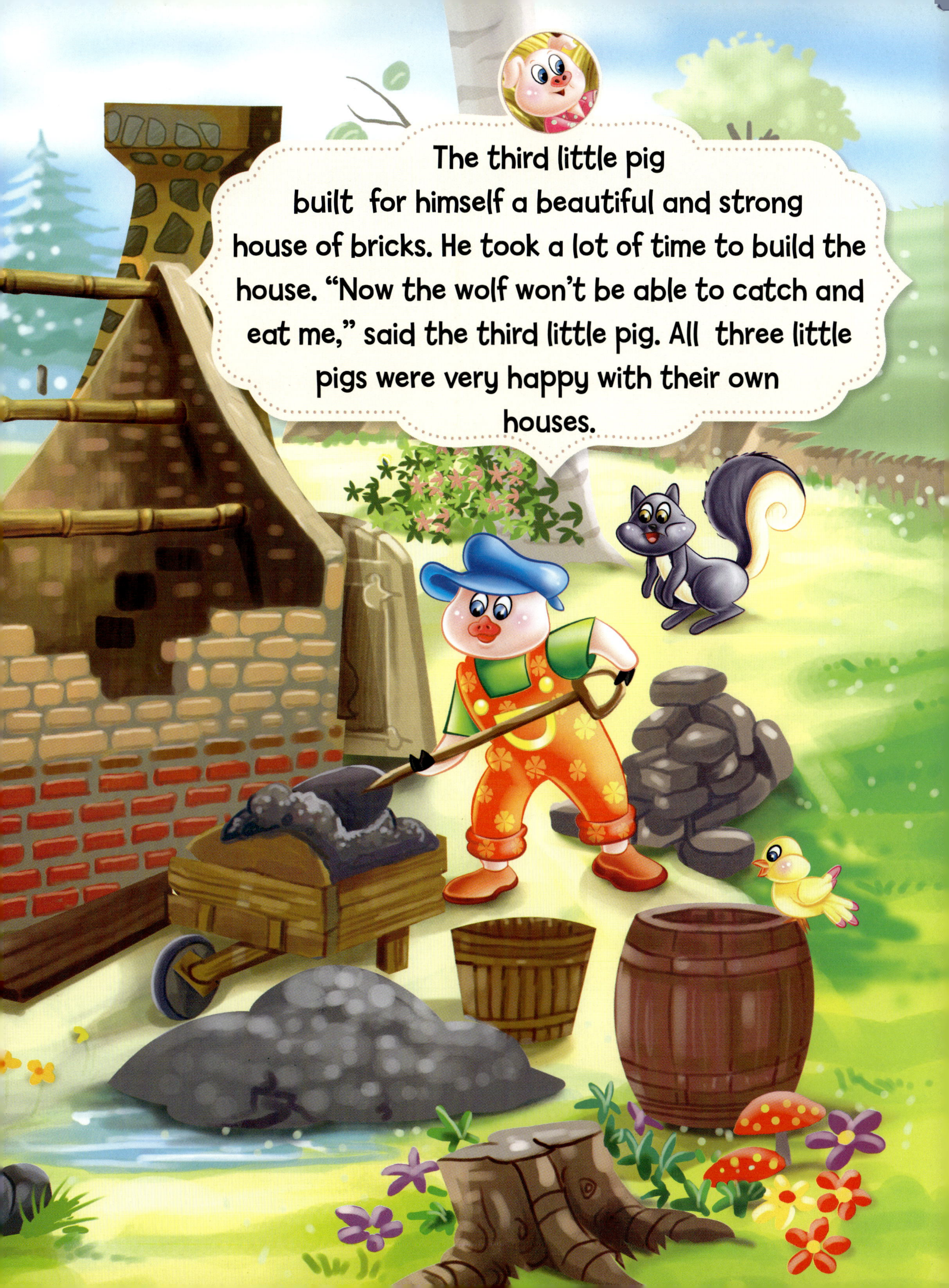

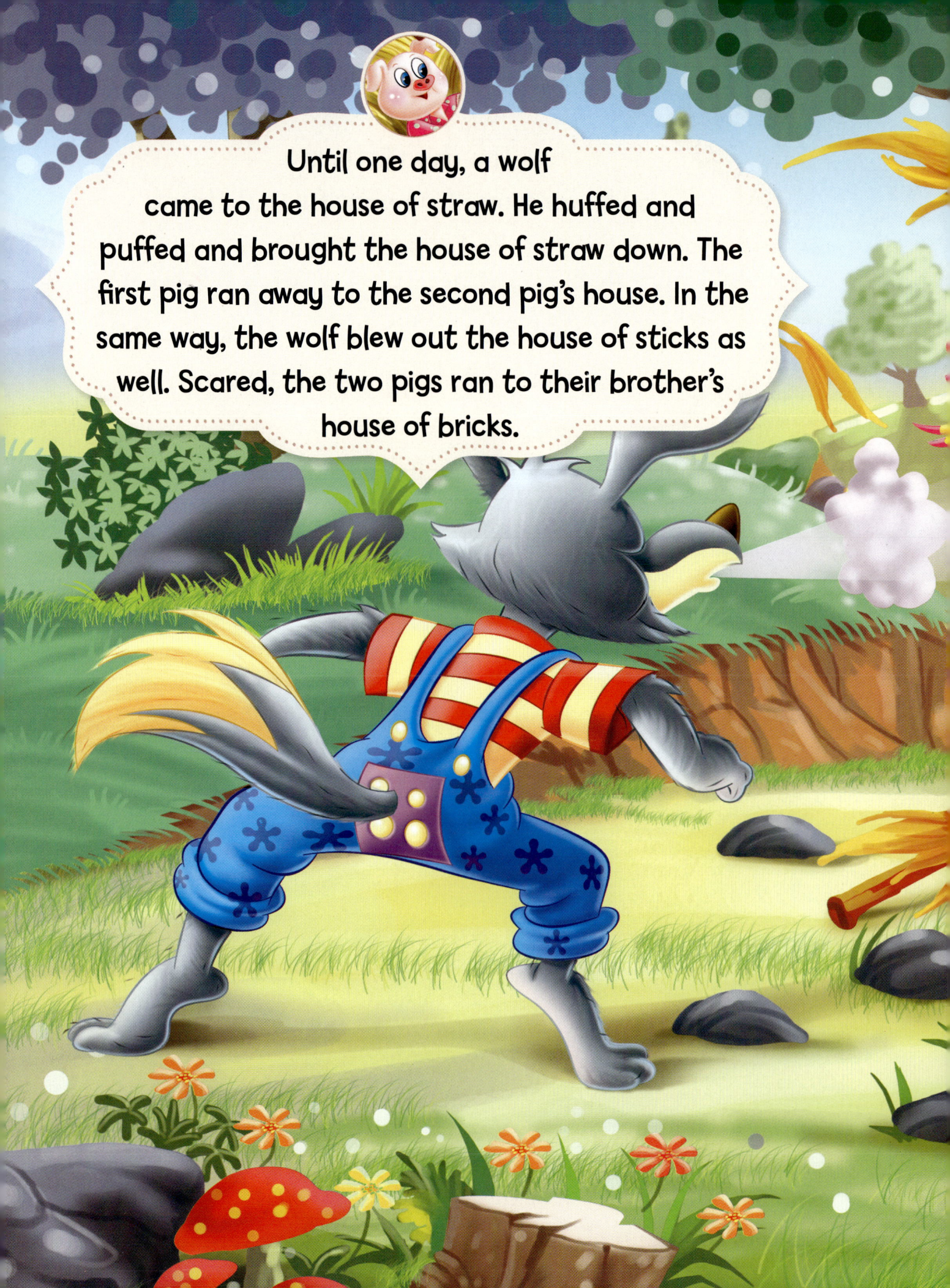

Until one day, a wolf came to the house of straw. He huffed and puffed and brought the house of straw down. The first pig ran away to the second pig's house. In the same way, the wolf blew out the house of sticks as well. Scared, the two pigs ran to their brother's house of bricks.

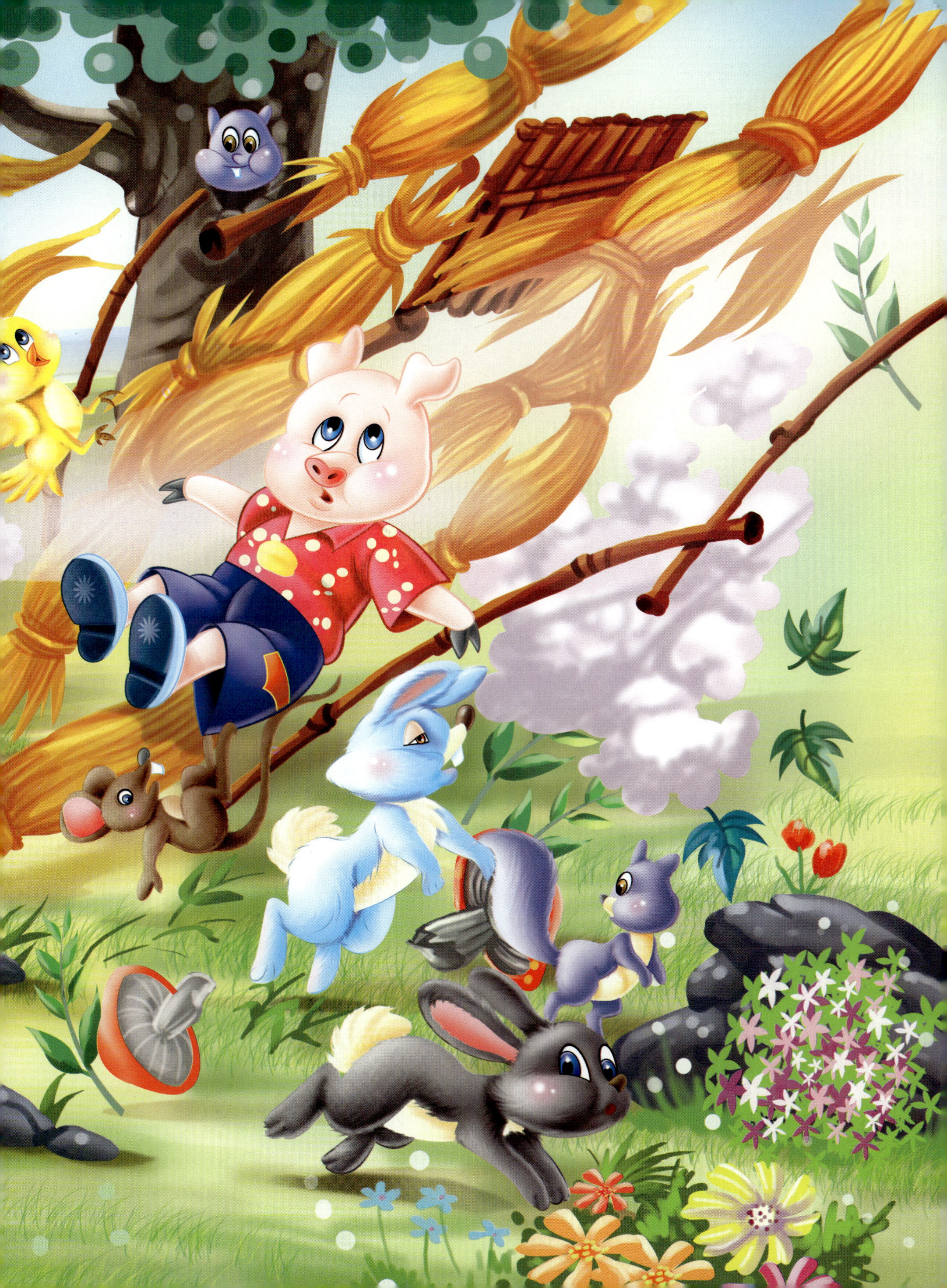

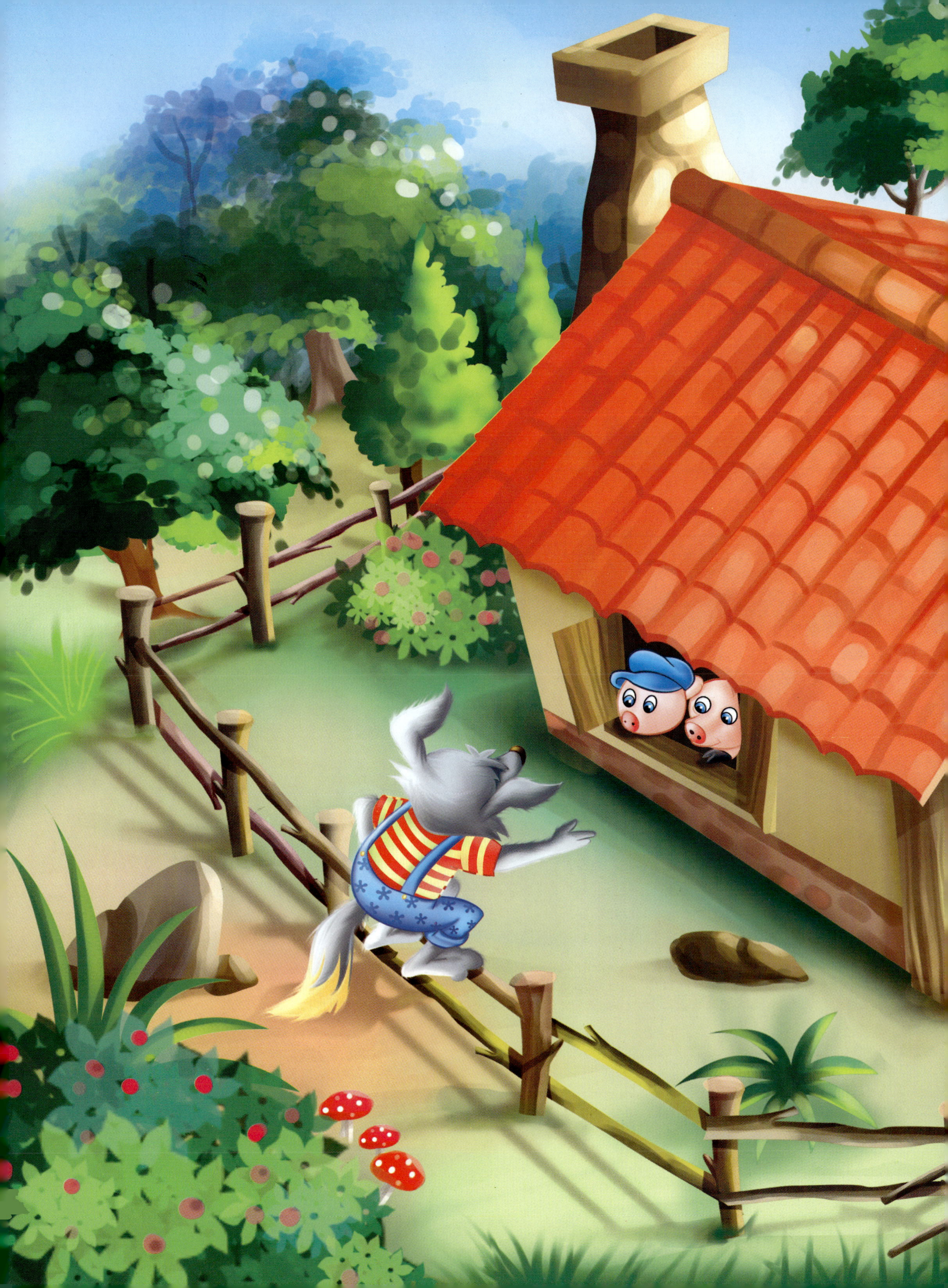

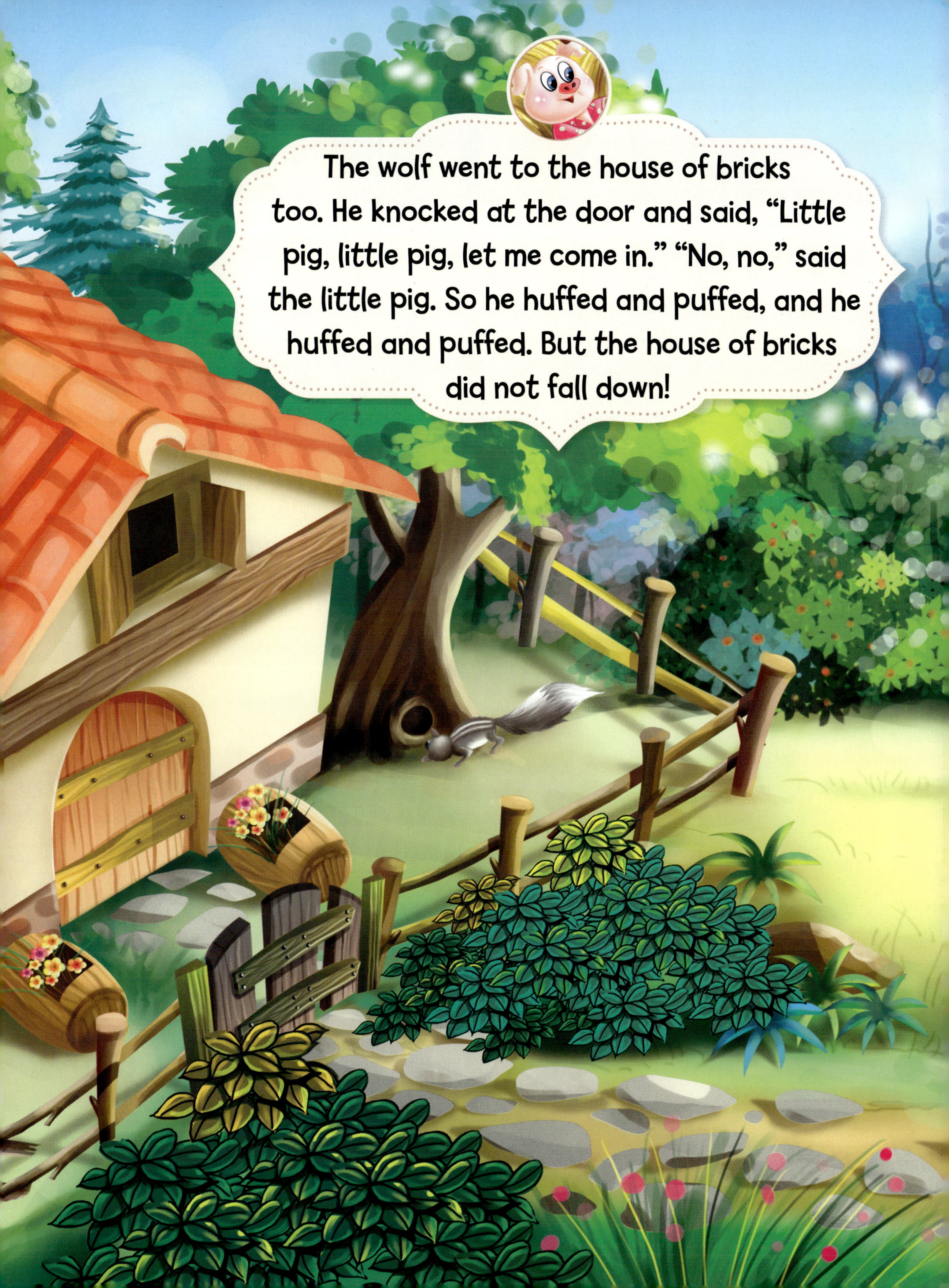

The wolf went to the house of bricks too. He knocked at the door and said, "Little pig, little pig, let me come in." "No, no," said the little pig. So he huffed and puffed, and he huffed and puffed. But the house of bricks did not fall down!

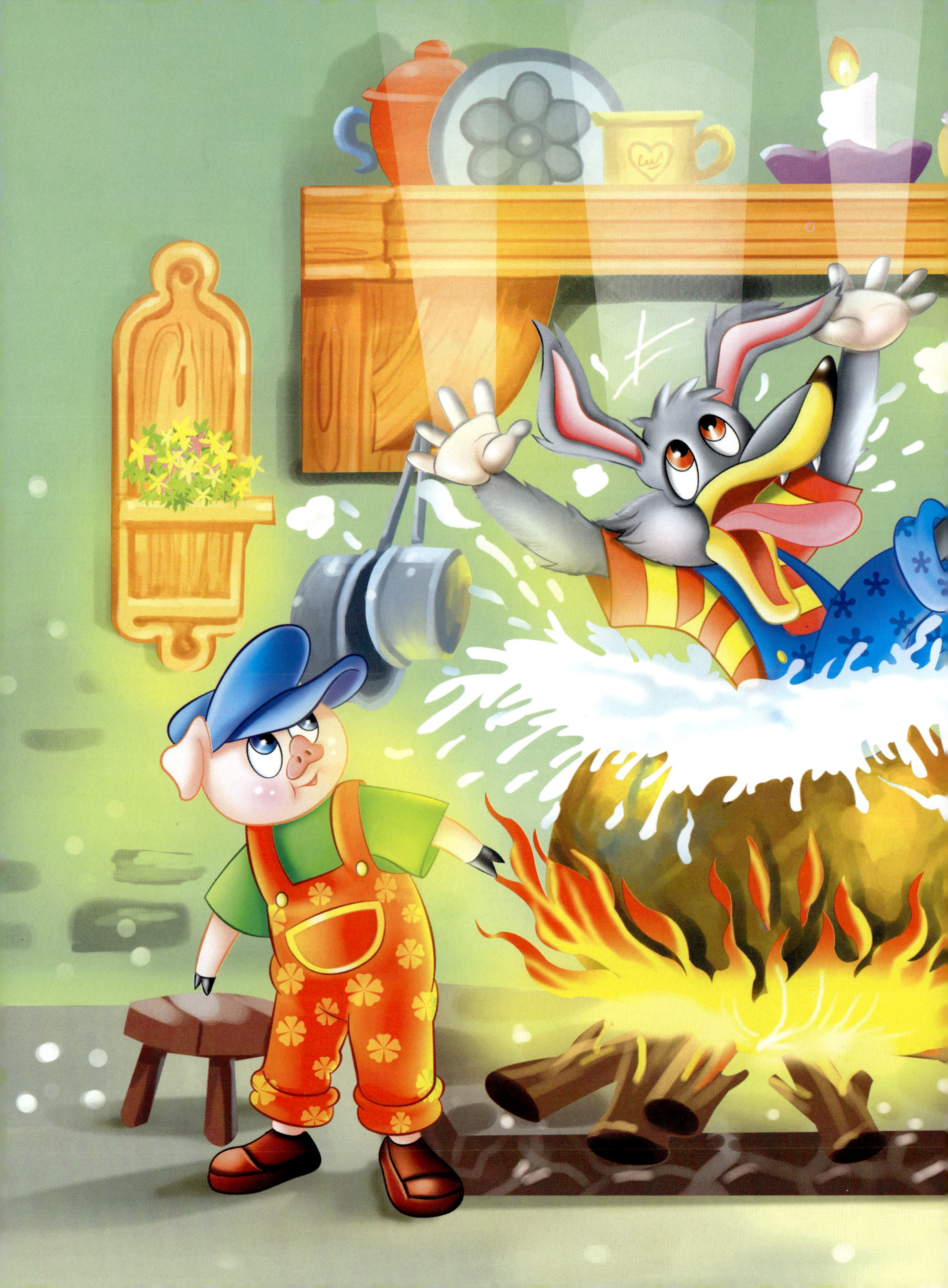

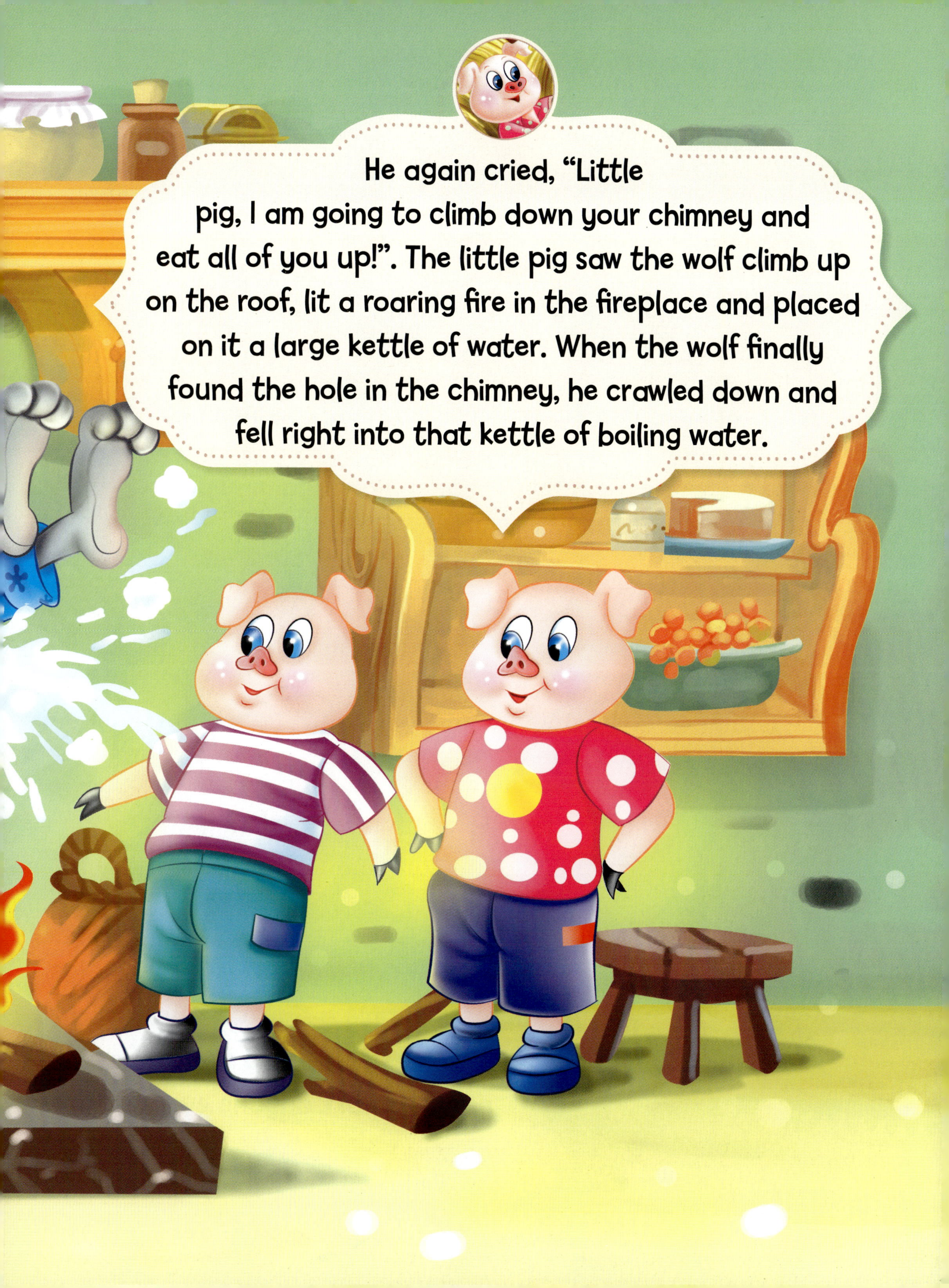

He again cried, "Little pig, I am going to climb down your chimney and eat all of you up!". The little pig saw the wolf climb up on the roof, lit a roaring fire in the fireplace and placed on it a large kettle of water. When the wolf finally found the hole in the chimney, he crawled down and fell right into that kettle of boiling water.

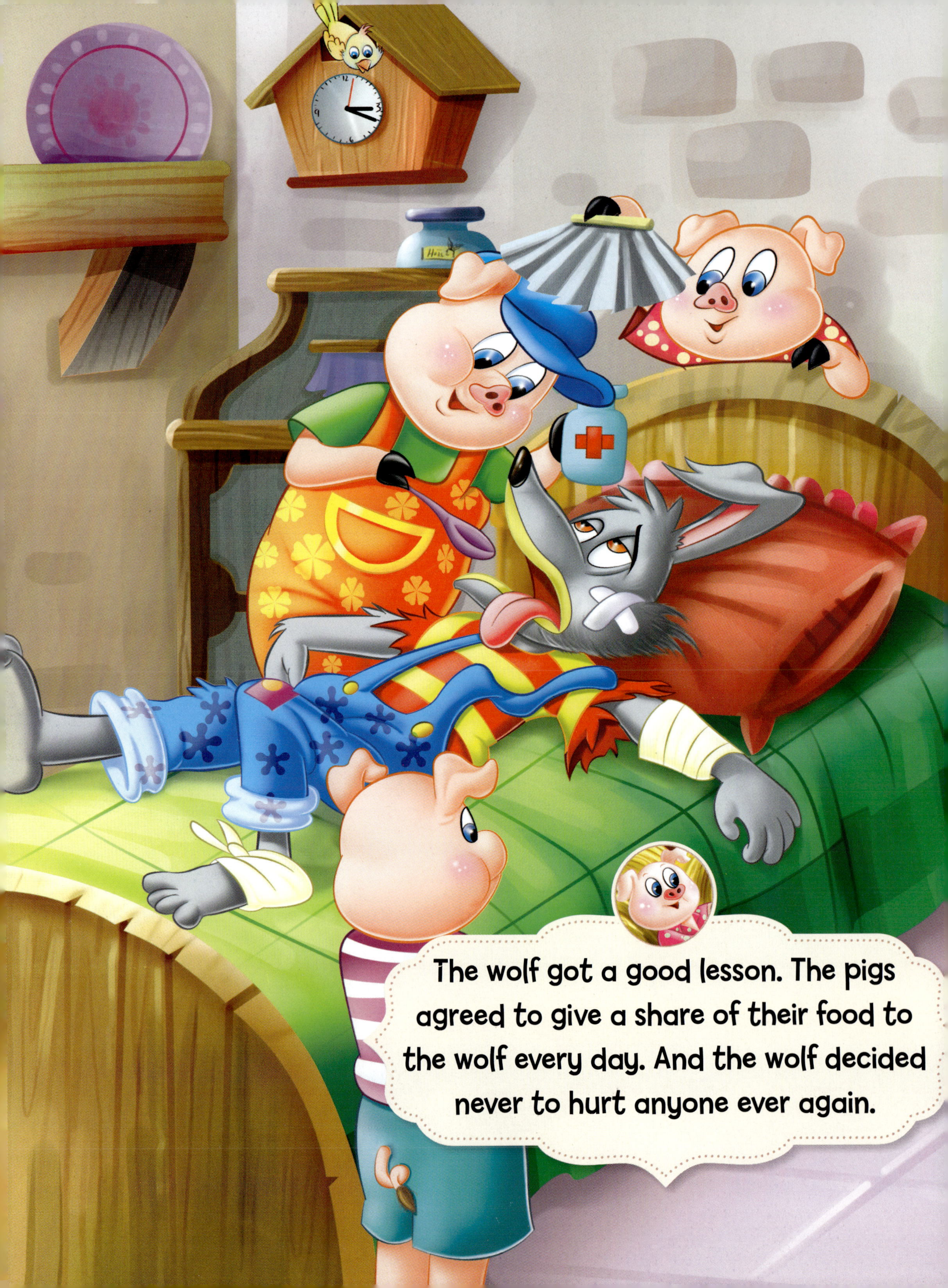

The wolf got a good lesson. The pigs agreed to give a share of their food to the wolf every day. And the wolf decided never to hurt anyone ever again.